THIS WALKER BOOK BELONGS TO:

_____

_____

_____

_____

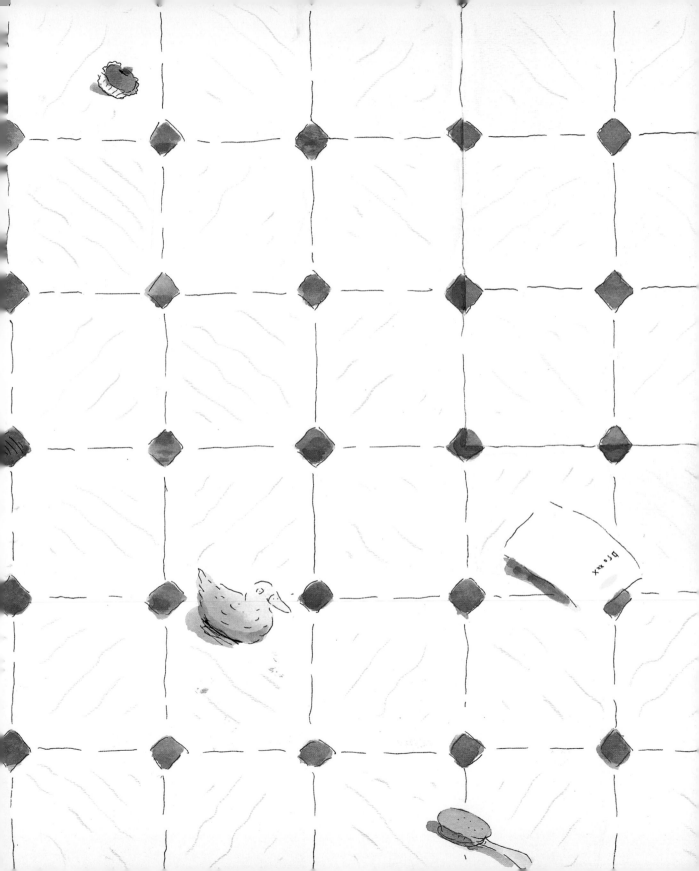

For Chloe and Theo

First published 1986 by
Walker Books Ltd
87 Vauxhall Walk
London SE11 5HJ

This edition published 1996

4 6 8 10 9 7 5 3

© 1986 Charlotte Voake

Printed in Hong Kong

British Library Cataloguing in Publication Data
A catalogue record for this book is available
from the British Library.

ISBN 0-7445-5272-9

TOM'S CAT

WRITTEN AND ILLUSTRATED BY

Charlotte Voake

WALKER BOOKS

AND SUBSIDIARIES

LONDON • BOSTON • SYDNEY

Here is Tom

looking for his cat.

CLICK CLICK CLICK

Is that Tom's cat
walking across the floor?

No. It's Grandma knitting socks again.

click click click

TAP TAP TAP

Is that Tom's cat?

Is he dancing on the table?

No.

Tom's mother is typing

a letter to her friend.

SPLASH SPLASH SPLASH

Is that Tom's cat?

No. Cats hate water.

So does Tom's brother.

But here he is,

trying to wash his hair.

CLATTER
CLATTER
CLATTER

What's that?

Is that Tom's cat
bringing everyone
a cup of tea?

No.

That's Tom's dad...

making pancakes.

And what's this loud noise?

VROOM

VROOM

VROOM

It sounds a bit like

Tom's cat on a...

MOTORBIKE!

VROOM
VROOM

But no.

It's Tom's sister

quickly cleaning the carpet

before anyone sees

she's dropped the cake

on the floor.

So where is Tom's cat?

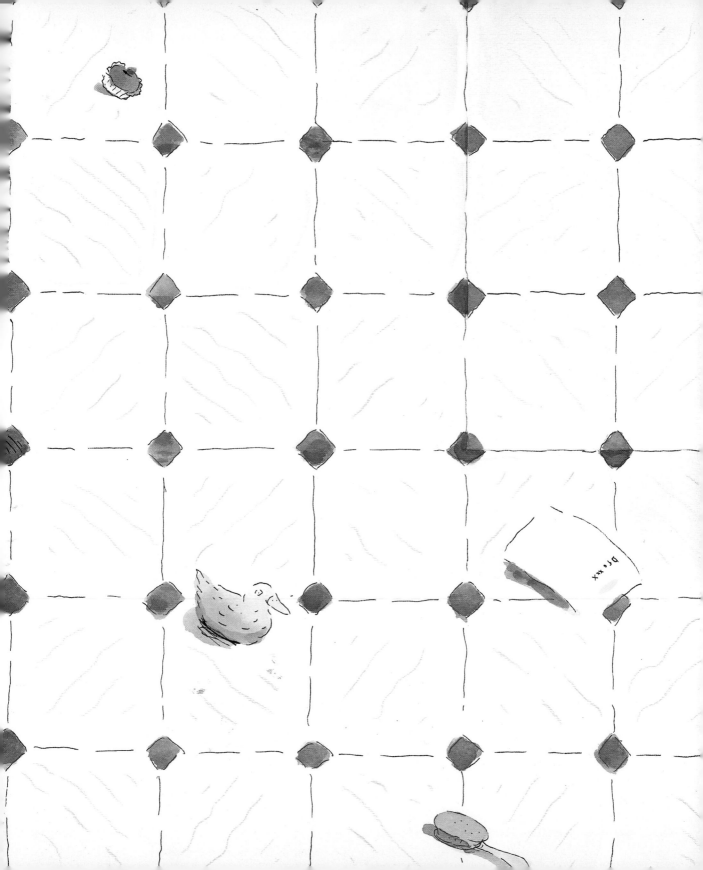

MORE WALKER PAPERBACKS
For You to Enjoy

Also by Charlotte Voake

GINGER
Winner of the Smarties Book Prize

Ginger is a very contented cat. He lives with a little girl who takes perfect care of him. But one day she brings home a surprise for Ginger that turns his blissful world upside down!

"As perfect a picture book for the very young as I can bring to mind."
Naomi Lewis, The Times Educational Supplement

0-7445-6035-7 £5.99

FIRST THINGS FIRST
Shortlisted for the Smarties Book Prize

This baby's companion has everything from ABC and 123 to nursery rhymes, fruits and insects.

"Every page is a surprise... This really is the book to catch your child's attention." *Young Mother*

0-7445-4709-1 £4.99

AMY SAID
written by Martin Waddell

"A triumph... Text and pictures work in harness as the children provoke one another to ever worsening behaviour. Understatement and lightness of touch couldn't find better exposition."
The Times Educational Supplement

0-7445-5227-3 £4.99